The
Mermaid's
Three Wisdoms

The Mermaid's Three Wisdoms

JANE YOLEN

ILLUSTRATIONS BY LAURA RADER

COLLINS WORLD

With special thanks to the following who helped with their own knowledge of the deaf child in our society:

The Louis Fischer family—Barbara and Valeria especially

Evelyn Glickman and her staff at the Willie Ross
School for the Deaf

Paul Oppenheim

Remy Charlip

Library of Congress Cataloging in Publication Data
Yolen, Jane H
The mermaid's three wisdoms.

SUMMARY: *A mermaid who cannot speak is banished from her undersea home and sent to live on land as a human where she is found by a twelve-year-old girl with a hearing impairment.*
(1. Physically handicapped—Fiction. 2. Friendship—Fiction. 3. Mermaids—Fiction) I. Rader, Laura.
II. Title.   PZ7.Y78Me   (Fic)   77-18325
ISBN 0-529-05420-5

Published by William Collins + World Publishing Co., Inc.
Cleveland • New York

For Heidi, who is wise in
her own way

The Three Wisdoms

1. Have patience, like the sea.
2. Move with the rhythm of life around you.
3. Know that all things touch all others,
   as all life touches the sea.

One

"It is dolphin weather," thought the mermaid. "It is for chasing whales and telling tales and exploring far beneath the sea."

She touched the old tortoise on the shell. His shell was hard and crisscrossed with scars, and her touch as light as a droplet. Though the tortoise looked too ponderous for games, he loved to play. He had been waiting for her to beckon, so he knew when her webbed fingers brushed his husk.

He followed her lead then. She swam with arms by her side, her tail making scant murmurs in the waves. He was close behind, graceful despite his bulk and age. He loved her as only a tortoise can, with patient distance, like a fond grandfather.

They were scarcely beyond the nearest reef when they were joined by a school of pout, then by a jetting squid. The procession was solemn at first, one after another. But the pout could not be restrained, and soon it was a full game of tag.

The mermaid Melusina leaped high into the air, laughing soundlessly at the squid who remained water-bound. She arched her back, flipped over, and landed with a splash not a yard off the port bow of a blue-and-white dinghy.

As she plunged downward, she realized with horror that she had been *seen*. There, in the dinghy, was a landgirl with hair caught up in two fat yellow braids. The girl was smiling.

Melusina hurried underwater to the water-carved grotto where she lived with her clan. She knew she must never be seen close up in the daylight by landfolk, but she had acted without thinking. It was her worst fault. Now, as each flash of her tail drove her deeper below the waves, she had only one hope. She swam frantically as if by putting the dinghy behind her, she could put the *seeing* behind her as well. She could feel her heart throbbing wildly in her breast and the pressure building up in her ears. She felt that she must hide away and forget what had been, make it exist no more.

But she was too late. The tattletale pout had gone ahead to tell the news to the merfolk. By the time Melusina reached her home, most of the clan had already gathered. They swayed by the side of the reef and spoke with their hands. Ripples formed soundlessly at their fingertips and spread their agitation to the top of the sea. But not before Melusina had understood.

There was anger there—and fear. Anger at her playful, unthinking violation of the laws; fear of what that violation might mean for them all.

"She has done it. This time she has really done it." The speaker was a merrowman named Dylan.

His squinty, little pigeyes narrowed to slits and his hands worked furiously. Anger was always communicated with the hands. The gentler emotions—shyness, happiness, and love—were usually formed in bubbles.

"The other things were annoyances. Hanging an anchor with a chain of pearls. Leaving a barnacled portrait on a boat's bottom. Mere pranks. Pranks that might have been done by the landfolk themselves—if they had the imagination. But this. *This!*"

His hands wrangled with one another in fury. Melusina was angry in return. Dylan, after all, was only newly come to their clan, having swum on a turbulent sea from Ireland in the last century. And everyone knew about the merrow and their tricks. What right had he to scold?

But Dylan's words were quickly picked up by the others. What could be worse than being sighted close up in this age of landscience when landfolk in shiny, black water clothes with rubber webbing on their feet and death sticks sometimes came hunting deep down in the sea, forcing the merfolk to seek refuge in the bottomless trenches and fault lines of the coast. In the old days, to be *seen* was a game played on unsuspecting sailors. But now all was changed. To be *unseen* was safe. To be *seen* was the deadliest threat to them all.

Hands moved ceaselessly: fear-waves rippled to the top with such vehemence, it surprised even the minnows. Never had such a commotion come from the merfolk within memory.

Melusina shivered as if caught in a sudden icy stream. What would they do to her? She had heard all their lectures before. The Three Wisdoms had been drummed into her since she was a tad: have patience; move with life's rhythm; know that all lives touch. It was difficult enough to remain still and listen while each adult member of the clan in turn gave essentially the same scolding. That was the punishment she hated. Not the lectures; she could always fog her eyes and not see them. But the immobility. To have to remain quiet, hands at her side, resting on her stilled tail, while the current pulled and called its siren song.

"It will be another boring lecture about the wisdoms and the rules," she said to her mother as she was led from the clan. She sighed. "That's it, isn't it?"

Her mother was silent, swimming by her side. "Melusina," she began suddenly, awkwardly turning to Melusina and stroking her daughter's hair, signing the name into the black strands. Then she fell silent again.

Melusina stood upright edgily on her wavering tail. Her mother, one of the gayest, most bubbling of the mermaids, was unusually still.

"Melusina," she began again, her fingers now on Melusina's arm, light filtering through the webbing that was already thickening with age. She stopped and turned away.

Melusina swam after, dove under, and came up before her mother. Then she began to reach out to touch her and stopped. Her mother was crying.

Melusina knew about the tears of merfolk from the tales they told, but she had never actually seen any of them cry.

At the corner of her mother's eye a crystal formed and then dropped slowly, turning over and over in the lazy current, burying itself at last in the sand.

"Mother," Melusina said, her fingers hard on her mother's shoulder, bubbles and hand sign merging in one desperate cry. "Mother, why are you crying? What is going to happen to me?"

Two

It was Dylan who had pushed them into a decision. He swam from one group of merfolk to another, touching them with his large-knuckled hands, punctuating each phrase with a pop of bubbles. And as he left each group, there was silence and staring. Then slowly, one after another, the merfolk fell in line behind Dylan and swam to the sea cave where Lir, their king, lived.

Lir was old, far older than any of them, and had once ruled the western seas of Ireland. But centuries earlier he had come to the uninhabited coast of New England in the hopes of leading a contemplative life. Some of the Scottish and Irish seafolk had followed him, mixing with the New World mermaids and mermen they found there.

The clan did not approach Lir with their usual politeness. They were upset, and so what came from them instead was a series of demands.

"She must be punished. She must go. She must have the Old Magic put on her." Dylan's wrangling hands cried it out first and the others signed their agreement. Hand upon hand around a hastily drawn-together circle, they followed Dylan's lead,

though few of them truly understood what Dylan meant.

Lir swam slowly in front of his cave, his shoulders encrusted with years of accumulated weeds and shells. He never brushed them off; his hands were usually too busy forming his thoughts, and if asked, he would have spoken slowly and with great passion of the need for merfolk to become even closer to their brothers and sisters of the sea. Lir's thoughts were always spun out of his hands with the slowest of motions.

"The Old Magic, my children?" He shook his head with the slightest of motions, hardly disturbing the eggs of a fish that lay jellied in his hair. "The Old Magic has not been used these four hundred years."

The oldest of the clan nodded, but Dylan alone pursued the argument. "And rightly. It has not been needed. The threat has been enough. The lectures and the implied threat. But this . . ." He left Melusina's misdeed unspoken, only suggested. And though all the merfolk knew what it was, had heard the pouts' report, Dylan's suggesting rather than speaking about the matter directly made it seem graver still.

Lir's tail barely moved. His gill slits opened and closed in somber rhythm. His eyes, deep purple with age, closed. For a long while he said nothing, and the merfolk waited with the patience of the sea.

At last he opened his eyes. There was great pain showing on his face. He said, "She is but a child."

The word he made with his hands was not exactly child, but "tad" crossed with the sign for "unschooled." And the sign meant both *untaught* and *without the help of her schoolmates.*

"Even a child can endanger us all. And is there not danger enough these days?" It was Dylan again, but this time the others joined in. Such words as "underwater ships" and "rubber swim bodies" and "the black oil slicks" bubbled furiously around Lir. Only Melusina's mother was still, her hands clasped wordlessly in front of her, so taut the webbing between her fingers was pulled nearly white. Her face spoke eloquently to Lir and he did not dismiss her plea.

At last the sea king stopped the merfolk with a look. Then he spoke in the old language; not only with his hands and with bubbles but with the seldom-used song sighs of the whale, the great sad singers of the sea.

"Listen well, then, my people, for what you ask is not easy. Harm is done to all when harm is done to one. Is that not the essence of the Third Wisdom? There is no one here who will escape if Melusina's mindlessness has revealed us to the landworld's eye.

"But we know the Third Wisdom works another way as well. For none of us can escape the consequences of what we choose to do to her in the name of our own safety. The Old Magic exacts a price for its use, a price that will be paid by our minds and our hearts. It may be a price that is too dear to pay.

"Yet if you so choose, I must obey. A sea king may counsel, but not command. A sea king is not master, but servant. What is your wish?"

Dylan shouted in a cascade of bubbles and hand signs, "The Old Magic."

The others followed, raising their hands above their heads and signing, "The Old Magic, the Old Magic."

Lir looked down at the sea bottom and sighed. Then he looked at the ring of merfolk. "Very well. Bring the tad. It shall be as you say. But you have forgotten the First Wisdom in your fear." He shook his head again and added, as if with great pain, "Bring Melusina here."

Then he swam back so slowly into his cave it seemed as if he did not move at all, but rather was carried in by a tide that was not felt by the others.

Barely had Lir disappeared into the cave's mouth when Dylan found Melusina. He grasped her harshly by an arm and pulled her through the water so quickly she did not have time to swim on her own. She had never thought of escaping, for where was there a place to escape to? From the corner of her eye she caught the movement of her tortoise friend, ever near, every hovering. She flicked him a nervous little hand sign as Dylan pulled her on. The merrowman thrust her through to the center of the circle of merfolk and swam to the edge to join them.

Within the circle, Melusina moved restlessly. She could not swim out. This was a double circle, the mermaids swimming parallel to the ocean bottom, the mermen vertically, all continually circling. It was unlike anything that Melusina had ever known her people to do. Only the tads were left out, and they floated uneasily above the adults, watching, their hands silent and fearfully still.

It was then that the great king Lir swam out of his cave, holding the largest conch Melusina had ever seen. She realized as she stared that she had only seen Lir twice in her life. He was older than she remembered, his beard down to his waist; and fiercer-looking, too. His shoulders were bent over with crustation, and there was a terrible sorrow on his face. Melusina looked out at him and tried to smile, to cheer him. She hated to see anyone feeling sad. That, strangely, made him sadder. She saw a crystal tear start in his eye; then the tear was washed down to the ocean bottom and buried in the sand.

"*Two* tears," Melusina thought suddenly. "Now there have been *two* crystal tears spent on me." She could wish a hundred more if they could change what she had done. She was suddenly afraid.

And then it began. The circles of merfolk swam faster and faster around and about her. As they gathered speed, they seemed to blur. The sea was churned by their movement. Melusina heard a horrible piercing cry as if a great cow whale had screamed above her. It came from Lir who was blowing on the conch, an ancient cry that echoed strangely under the water. Then he lowered the shell and began to speak in signs and bubbles:

> *From the sea sever her,*
> *From the sea deliver her,*
> *Cast away, cast away, cast away.*

The circle of merfolk joined him, crying in the old tongue: "Cast away, cast away, cast away."

Melusina felt a great searing pain in her tail as if it were cleft in two. Suddenly she could no longer breathe. Gasping, she reached up to her gill slits, fearing they were blocked. Her hands touched her neck, behind her jaw, under her ear, but the slits were gone. It could not be, yet it was.

The world went black, then searingly white, and she knew no more.

Three

Jasmine Merchant was the girl in the dinghy. Jasmine—Jess. She wore her hair in two braids only when she was off rowing by herself or with Captain A., the old whaling captain who lived by himself on Shelter Isle. With her hair in two braids, her hearing aid showed, and Jess would allow no one to see it and feel sorry for her. Captain A. never noticed it, or if he did, he never spoke of it.

In school, even at home, she wore her hair down over her ears with a fierceness that earned her a reputation as a stubborn, angry child. She had no close friends, for she snubbed the "hearing" children at her new normal school. She had snubbed the totally deaf ones at her old school— the special school—in the same manner, refusing to sign with them except when forced to in class. Even her own mother found her a difficult child, though she continually assured Jess of her love. But Jess reached out to no one, offered none of the hugs and touches that reassure others of affection. She felt herself unique, caught as she was between the two worlds, neither all deaf nor all hearing. So she had friends in neither world. To make a friend one needed words, and Jess regarded words as slippery, untrustworthy things that slid off your hands or out of your mouth, dangerous as eels.

Jess thought about her morning. She had left home angry as usual, but still her mother had let her go. The doctors all advised that a child with an *impairment* (how Jess hated that word; it made her feel damaged, like a broken toy brought home from the store in pieces) should be encouraged to be "an independent and active participant in life." That's what it said in one of the innumerable pamphlets and books about deafness they had in the house. So Jess's mother encouraged her to be independent. In fact it sometimes felt to Jess as if her mother practically threw her out of the house at every opportunity.

Also, Jess's mother made a great big *thing* about her deafness. She always said, "Jess, you're so much brighter than most hearing-impaired children." Funny, thought Jess, how she never says *deaf*. "It should be your mission, Jess, to help others *more* unfortunate. . . ." She had said it again that very morning. Actually what Jess really wanted to do was to forget her deafness. Because it made her so angry, so very, very angry.

But here, on the sea, she couldn't remain angry long. Jess let the motion calm her down once again. And it was then, when she was totally calm and relaxed, that the mermaid surfaced, leaped, flipped over, and disappeared.

Jess was not altogether surprised. She believed that the sea—her sea—held all kinds of miracles. One more couldn't really surprise her. It just filled her with a quiet delight.

Every day, even in the cold fall and early spring, she rowed out in her blue-and-white dinghy into Murdock Harbor just waiting for such surprises. She was never disappointed. She had seen dolphins breaking the water, lazy skates, and one special large old tortoise she could identify by the crossways scars on his shell. And three times this year she had seen some unidentifiable kind of whales spouting far off against the horizon. And now this.

This was something to tell Captain A. She would share it with him and no one else. For he was so like her, living apart from the rest of the world. And, after all, he shared occasional stories with her, stories of the old whaling days off Nantucket. Tales of the time when pirates hunted the Maine coast. Tales of ghosts haunting those same coasts today: old Babb, the butcher of Appledore, and the lovely lily maid of Smuttynose waiting for her husband, the dreaded pirate Blackbeard, to return.

The captain always spoke slowly and loudly, not because he pitied her deafness, but because that was the way he spoke to everyone. Slowly and loudly. Maybe he was partly deaf himself, hard of hearing just like Jess. But he wouldn't give in to it. Not him. He did without a hearing aid. And when Jess was with him, she could gladly take hers off.

The captain spoke loudly and slowly and lovingly of the things on the sea, and she watched and listened carefully to all he said without the agony of guessing if she had gotten it correct. He demanded few words from her in return.

He would love to know she had seen a mermaid. A mermaid leaping out of the foam with a scaly tail and hair in salty tangles and a mouth pursed in horrified surprise.

Just wait till I see him, Jess thought with delight. She put her oars back into the water. Then singing "Haul Away Joe," Captain A.'s favorite short drag chanty, she pulled weightily on the oars toward Shelter Isle.

Her monotone song went right into a kind of babbling, a private conversation she kept with herself. "Mermaids are myths," she said. To her own ears her voice was soft, even melodic, but to others it sounded thick and loud and flat. "Myths are not real, and what I saw was very real. So maybe it wasn't a mermaid. Or maybe"—and she gave the oars a particularly hard pull—"maybe mermaids *aren't* myths!"

She stopped talking then because her own voice had drowned out every other sound. And she wanted to hear the sea. It was an answer all in itself, a sound she could always distinguish even without her hearing aid, because it was a deep vibration in her entire body. There was nothing slippery about it. It was the most solid and real thing in her life. She felt the *pit-swash, pit-swash* as the waves licked the boat. Now that single sound was like a voice inside her, a voice that told her that anything was possible in the sea—even mermaids.

The dinghy scraped on the sandy beach of the small island and rocked her back and forth. She recovered in an instant and leaped out of the boat, unmindful of the cold water on her sneakers and pants. Her clothes were always damp and full of salt and sand. Her mother complained about it, but it never bothered Jess. She hauled the dinghy far enough up onto the beach to anchor it, for the tide was going out anyway. Then she took off at a soft canter across the dunes toward the island's center where the captain's shack lay sheltered in the pines.

"Captain A.," she hollered against the wind. "Captain A., ahoy." The words came back to her, thick and muddy.

As she came over the final dune, she could see no one near the tar-paper and grey-shingle shack. But smoke was coming from the large, battered oil drum that stood on four legs by the front door. Jess knew that meant the captain was cooking a lobster, and if that were so, he would not be far away.

"Ahoy," she yelled again.

"Ahoy yerself," came a loud, growling reply as a grizzled old man hobbled out. He limped slightly, and a small wind made his thin white hair halo out around his head. Jess saw him speak before she registered his words.

"Always come at dinner, do ye?" he said with a slow smile. He punctuated it with a sketchily signed question mark. Someone else might think there was anger in his gruff words and the quick hand sign, but not Jess.

Jess smiled back at him and said nothing.

"Well, it's a small 'un. Not big enough for a twelve-year-old mermaid. Just a quick nibble for an old man."

"That's all right. I'm not hungry," said Jess. She knew the old man had barely enough for himself. "I really came 'cause I have a secret to tell you. A surprise."

"*Argh*, you're just wanting some of me dinner. A secret for a bite. I know you young 'uns. Always like to trick an old man."

"I'd never trick you, Captain," said Jess as he ruffled her hair with a rough hand. She sat down on the sand near the lobster barrel and crossed her legs. The sand stuck to her damp trousers and shoes.

"So, what is this secret, gel?" the old man asked. He peered nearsightedly into the barrel at the cooking lobster.

"I saw a . . . ," said Jess, and then the words failed her. She grimaced and instead made the signs for fish and for girl in the hand signs she had been taught at the special school. It held bad memories for her, that hand speech, of faces on the street filled with pity as the students walked between classes and the cafeteria, chattering silently. She rarely used it—except with Captain A. to whom she had taught a few words in exchange for his showing her how to semaphore with flags. But

Captain A. had never picked up the finger spelling well. His hands were arthritic and slow, clumsy, and old. Besides, he had no trouble understanding her speech. Not like some. Sometimes, though, they used signing as a game between them.

"A fish, you say." The captain laughed. "Seen plenty today meself."

Jess shook her head and signed again, smiling. "Fish," her hands said and then, linking it, "girl."

The old man turned to look at his pot again, then back to Jess. "I saw some fine eating fish when I was out getting me lobster."

"Not a fish. A *mermaid*," Jess shouted as if she had played the greatest joke on the old man.

"Did ye."

"With a fish tail. And . . . and sea anemones"— she had to stumble over the last word—"in her hair. And a pearldrop necklace, too. She was naked. She jumped not a foot off my port bow." For Jess it was a very long speech.

"Did ye?"

"I think she was surprised."

"I'd be surprised, too. *If* I thought it was true."

"*Captain!*" Jess was stunned. She had never heard this tone from him before.

He looked straight at Jess and spoke loudly and deliberately, his mouth working hard to shape his message. "The sea is too wonderful to be improved upon by you, Jess gel. I thought you knew that. The tales I tell, about the ghosts and the revenants and the haunts along the Isles of Shoals, well there's some that believes 'em, I guess. But you and me, we know the real wonders that lie out on the sea. No need to pretty 'em up."

"But I did see her. *I did*."

"No doubt you did, gel. In your heart of hearts. But in your eye, now, what you saw was a porpoise a-leapin' up or a turtle flippin' his foot at ye." The old man let his hands illustrate. "Don't I know? Eighty-four years, boy and man, I been on the sea. And they *are* wonders. Every last one of 'em."

But Jess would not be changed. "I was this close," she said, holding her hands apart.

"That's hardly a foot, gel. More like a hand. Begone with ye. I'm in no mood for sech." The old man turned his back and gaffed the lobster with his long fork.

Jess was stunned. "Only *some* of it was a story," she said, pulling out the admission like a splinter from flesh. "The anenomes and the pearl necklace weren't true. But she *was* a mermaid. And she was as naked as . . . as . . ." The words failed her again. All she could do was whisper, "I swear it. I swear it."

But the captain had gone into his shack without another word. His door slammed behind him, punctuating his wordless good-bye. Jess could feel its force.

Her mouth was left ajar. She closed it angrily. "Bet he wishes he had seen it first," she thought savagely to herself. And thinking this, she dropped to her knees and drew a mermaid in the sand by the lobster pot. Then she got up and stomped over the dunes to her boat.

Four

The dinghy was well beached by now, for the tide was out. Jess was angry at the thought of having to drag the boat so far. And she was angry with the captain, too. Why hadn't he taken a moment to listen, to believe?

As she stomped over the last dune, she saw the dinghy and something else close by it. A figure. Someone lying in the sand.

Jess ran the rest of the way down to the boat, screaming as she went, "Are you all right? Are you all right?" The words blurred together into a single ragged cry. Jess was frightened, really frightened. Drownings were not all that uncommon. She had read just last week in the local paper about someone being washed up along shore.

When she got closer, she saw it was a girl, lying face down in the sand. Her blue-black hair spun out around her like a webbing. She had no clothes on and did not seem to be breathing.

As Jess leaned over, she could not help noticing the blue-green tinge of the skin on the girl's arms and back. But her legs were soft-looking and white, as if they had never been touched by the sun. Jess wondered briefly if the girl were crippled.

She hesitated a minute, conquered her fluttering stomach, then touched the girl's back with the palm of her hand. The body was wet, cool, even clammy. But the girl could not have been on the beach long. Perhaps she was not dead.

Remembering with a rush all the lifesaving skills from the lessons her mother had insisted on as a price for the dinghy, Jess straddled the body. She pulled the girl's face to the side, put her arms up over her head and began pushing.

"Out goes the bad air, in comes the good," Jess repeated over and over, remembering what the out-loud repetitions of that simple phrase had cost her at swimming lessons. The other children, seeing her without her hearing aid, did not know she was deaf. They had mocked her voice, calling her "Mushmouth," until the instructor had stopped them. But none of them, she bet, had ever had a chance to *really* save someone from drowning. She pressed down, released, pressed down, released.

It seemed like ages. She tried not to think that the girl might be dead already, that she was handling a dead body. She made herself think only of the rhythm.

"Out goes the bad air," she muttered, looking again at the blue-black hair in front of her. She had never seen hair such a beautiful dark color. "In comes the good air." Jess looked at the girl's hands that were spread out in the sand. There was a light-colored flap of skin between each finger.

"Oh, my lord," said Jess aloud; and just then the

girl's legs stiffened in one convulsive movement, and she gave a harsh, frothy cough.

Jess got off the girl's back and tried to turn her over. As she did so, the girl flipped over on her own and stared full into Jess's eyes.

It was the mermaid.

Confused, Jess backed away. She looked again at the girl, shaking her head. It was a stranger, of course. No one Jess had ever seen in Murdock. Not a mermaid but a human. Perhaps she had been drowning when Jess had seen her, trying to leap free of the pull of the tide. Perhaps . . . but her perhapses seemed lame, even to Jess. And when the girl tried to rise up and her legs collapsed like rubber under her, Jess simply went over and put her arms around the other girl, who turned her face silently against Jess's shirt.

At last, though, Jess put her hand under the girl's chin and looked again at her face. Though the girl had seemed to be sobbing, she was completely dry-eyed.

"Who are you?" Jess worked hard at getting the syllables right.

The girl from the sea was silent.

"Where are you from?"

Still the girl didn't answer, but this time she held her hands over her ears and made a face as if Jess's voice hurt her.

That made Jess furious. She hated any reminder that her speech was imperfect. "Well, I was just trying to help. I just saved your life, in case you've forgotten."

The girl kept her hands to her ears, and Jess

screamed at her then: "Listen to me, you. I just saved you." She reached over to grab the girl's hands from her ears, and the girl started back like some wild creature. As she moved, her black hair fell behind her shoulders, and Jess saw a series of three bright red lines on the side of her neck. It looked as if someone had taken a knife to her— and recently.

"Oh," said Jess, "You poor thing." Her anger was forgotten at once. The girl must have been cruelly treated, perhaps knifed, maybe even beaten, thrown into the sea to drown. In her pity for the other girl, Jess brushed a few remaining tendrils of hair from the girl's neck. The girl trembled like an animal unused to a human touch, but did not move again.

"How did it happen?" Jess asked, but her fingers answered her, for as she ran them lightly down the lines she realized how smooth the other's neck was. These weren't scars, mutilations, something new. They were a part of her, somehow, like a birth-mark. Thoughtfully, Jess looked at the other side of the girl's neck. She did not try to touch her again. The same three red lines were there, too.

The girl began to tremble more, put her hands over her eyes, and bent over from the waist. Her hair fell around her like a dark curtain.

Jess suddenly felt ashamed. She had been treating the girl like a freak, a curio, like a piece in a museum, the way other people treated Jess. "Look, I'm sorry. You must be, well, going into shock. Here." She stood up and went to the dinghy,

got her sweater, and put it around the girl's shoulders. "I'll be right back. I'm going to get a grownup. He'll know what to do. Now don't move. Don't . . ."

Without finishing the sentence, Jess began to back away from the girl, her hands in front of her, signing and finger spelling in her anxiety to communicate. Anything to get the other girl to understand her. Then suddenly she turned and ran over the dune toward the center of the island to the shack that nestled in the low pines. She glanced back at the beach only once.

Once the landgirl had left, Melusina flung the scratchy covering from her. It landed in the water and floated there. The covering had neither the deep salt smell nor the flow of water to it. She could not bear it touching her skin. Yet she was cold, colder than she had ever been in her life. And afraid.

The other girl, the landgirl, was so strange. Her body was covered all over with rough seaweedy material. The nightmare sounds the girl made with her mouth were horribly grating on her ears. And she had no gills. But worst of all was the way she looked right at Melusina. Looked at her, stared, watched every move. To be *seen* by a landgirl was wrong. Yet Melusina could not get away from that girl's strange, staring eyes.

Melusina tried to piece together what had happened. It was the Old Magic, of course. She had only heard of it once or twice, and then it was always spoken of with loathing. The Old Magic, the ability to change shape. Changing into things not of the sea—or into one of the horrors of the deep. No self-respecting member of the clan wanted to be other than mermaid or merman. When the merfolk had come from the old lands to the new, where shape-changing was all but unknown, the followers of Lir had given up the Old Magic. Or so she had been told. Only Lir, the king, still knew the words, still knew the signs, still knew the spells. And he had been forced to use it on her.

But what good did all that knowledge do her, now, a castaway from her own? Melusina looked around. Much less than a league away lay the sea, her beloved home. She tried to get up and go to it. Only then did she *really* understand. She could not even sit with ease. She looked down and saw. She had no tail. Two white limbs sprang from her body. She had legs like the landfolk. These two detestable legs—they would keep her from her sea. She would never be able to go back now.

Melusina began to cry. A crystal tear formed in the corner of one eye and dropped with a gentle sound beside her in the sand. Angrily she picked it up and flung it toward the ocean. As it dropped, turning over and over in the air, she made the sign with her hand for *hatred*. But the sign was so close in its fingering to the hand sign for *love* that her meaning was indistinct. She watched the crystal tear drop out of sight, gulped down into the maw of the sea. Perhaps, just perhaps, her mother would find it and know whose it was. Perhaps, just perhaps, she would care.

A great turtle humped up out of the sea, his shell crisscrossed with scars. He raised his beak and in it, held gently yet firmly, was the crystal teardrop. But Melusina was too deep in her own dark misery to notice, and the tortoise sank back again in a moment and swam away.

Five

"Captain A. Oh, please, Captain A.," screamed Jess as she came toward the shack.

The old seaman was outside his grey house eating the lobster, and looked up with mild surprise. Jess was usually a much quieter, more deliberate child. She rarely spoke, much less yelled. With an old man's forgetfulness, he did not remember their earlier quarrel.

"There's a . . ." Jess was so out of breath, she had trouble remembering how to form her words. And when they finally came, tumbling over one another in her anxiety, they mixed together like a poorly blended chowder. "An almost drowned girl on the beach . . . helped her . . . she's breathing." Here she herself had to stop for breath.

The captain stood up at once, not even waiting to hear the rest of the story.

Jess had time for the warning: "But she hasn't any clothes on."

"Poor tad," the old man said. It was what he always called a child he felt sorry for, though he had never once called Jess that, to her undying gratitude. "Poor little tad." He went into his shack and came out with a sheet and blanket. The sheet was dirty and smelled of fish. The blanket was a dark blue.

The two of them ran back over the sand, Jess in the lead. The captain, because of his bad leg, was slower and breathed heavily as he ran.

Jess tried to look back over her shoulder and tell the rest of the story as they went. It caused her to stumble every few steps, and so her story, too, stumbled. It came out in key words, thin and unrecognizable. "Lines. Webs. White legs."

The captain, intent on saving his own breath for the trip, did not answer her.

When they clambered over the last dune, Jess almost expected the strange girl to be gone. But she was still there, looking out over the sea, half sitting and half lying down, her legs stiff and uncomfortable-looking.

Jess called out eagerly as they came down the side of the dune, but the girl did not seem to hear, just kept her silent vigil over the ebbing tide. It wasn't until the captain touched her shoulder that she turned her head to look at them.

"Here now, tad, wrap this around ye," the old man said. He bent down as he spoke and looked into the girl's sea-black eyes. There was a tenderness in his attitude that Jess did not altogether like. She preferred him gruff and laughing.

The girl, though she was naked, tried to shove the sheet away from her, but she shivered perceptibly as she did so. The captain wrapped it firmly around her and, with a great grunt, stood up with her in his arms.

"Quick, Jess, me gel, put the blanket over her. Why you left her here freezing, I cannot say. You should have wrapped her before coming screaming for me."

"But I did! I did!" Jess cried out. She could hear her own voice rising, getting harsher, filling the air with an incredible whine. "I gave her my sweater. I did! I did!"

But the captain had already turned with the girl in his arms, adjusting the blanket over her and crooning comfortingly with soft, liquid sounds that Jess could not distinguish no matter how hard she tried. So instead she had to trudge after them, anger and disappointment churning inside.

The covering the old man put on her was softer than the scratchy thing the girl had left. And it smelled deliciously of the sea. Melusina snuggled down inside it and closed her eyes. If she tried, she could even forget where she was.

Except that there was no pull of the current along her body. There was no washing of the water through her gill slits. There was no swaying movement of her tail. There was no soft twilight of the undersea world, the quiet murmurations of the tide.

Here, in the upper world, the world of land, everything was too bright, too loud, too harsh. Everything hurt her eyes, and ears, and skin, and mind. Lights and sounds beat upon her. Every

touch of air or sand or covering seemed to scrape raw places on her flesh. It was an ugly world up here, static and coarse, and she hated it at once. Before, she had only had glimpses when she leapt free of the sea, or when she sat at midnight on a rock tickling the soft underbelly of a newborn seal, or when she pulled herself along an anchor chain and stared into a ship through the rounded holes. And those glimpses of land life had been exciting when she knew she would, seconds later, be back in the pulsing world of the ocean. But to be left forever on the land was not exciting at all. It was horrible.

The sounds and the light suddenly seemed to mute, and Melusina dared to open her eyes. They were in some kind of cave, a dwelling place. Furtively she looked around. In all the wealth of new things, she saw some that were familiar: an anchor, a shark's jaw, a piece of whalebone with strange markings on it, bits of coral and shells.

Suddenly she ached to touch something of the sea. She untangled her hands from the covering. She could not make bubbles, and so she signed with her hands that she would like to touch something. But neither the bearded old one nor the girl seemed to listen.

Melusina signed again and again, but it was impossible to talk to them. They did not, would not, hear.

It was suddenly too much to bear. Melusina put her head on her arm and began to weep the silent sobs of the sea.

Jess looked at the sea girl and saw that she was gesturing. It was obvious to her that the girl wanted something, but the movements she was making with her hands were strange. They were like Jess's own hand signs only somehow in a different language altogether. Jess could almost—but not quite—understand them.

"She wants something."

The captain shrugged. "She wants something to eat, I'll wager. Some broth. I'll make it." He went over to his wood stove and stoked up its coals.

Jess shook her head. "No, she wants something on your shelf."

"Not my prizes. No!" The old man bit his cracked lip. He never let anyone touch his things, though he had told Jess many tales about each of them.

But the sight of the girl who had been drawn from the sea gesturing, mourning, moved him. When she put her head on her arm, he stepped forward. She was crying, not like Jess or the other children he had known, but rather silently, heavily, hopelessly. It was her silent grief that decided him. He limped over to her and lifted her head from her arm, and then he stared.

Falling from one of her eyes was the most beautiful crystal he had ever seen.

He took a step back. "Lord help us!" he said. "It's a mermaid!"

Six

Now it was Jess's turn to be startled. Now that the captain had actually said the word, made the judgment, she could not believe it.

"You said," she began loudly and carefully to the old man's back, "you said that the sea was wonderful enough without such stories. You said . . ."

But the captain was not listening. "Lord, help us," he repeated. "Look at her eyes. Look at her tears. The stories, the tales, they're true. All true. Mermaids cry crystal tears, they say. And there it is." He put his arm around the sea girl and crooned, "There, there, my pretty tad. Old Captain A. will help ye."

But behind his back, Jess did not hear him. Without the movement of his lips to guide her, she did not know what he was saying. All she saw was the white head bent over the blue-black one, the hairy arm over the smooth shoulders of the girl, the captain—her captain—murmuring into the salt-tangled web of the other girl's hair.

Something hurt inside her. A strange sound she did not recognize pushed from her mouth. She turned and ran out of the cabin, slammed the door as hard as she could, and ran over the dunes to the beach. There she found her boat and beside it her sweater in a small tide pool. She sat down by the water's edge and began to sob. Not silent, tearless sobs like the mermaid's but great, loud, gasping, retching sobs that drowned out every other sound in her head, even the sound of the sea.

Inside the dwelling place, the old man had taken the conch shell off his shelf and laid it like an offering in Melusina's lap. He took the crystal tear in exchange. Melusina did not mind the loss of the tear. But she stroked the shell lovingly, as if it were some kind of pet. She did not cry again.

As she watched, the old man bustled around the darkened place, making shuffling sounds and occasionally glancing over at her. She was reminded of her old tortoise friend, for the man looked at her with the same small liquid eyes. She might have compared him with Lir, for they both had beards and white hair. But this old one had none of Lir's fierce, sorrowing majesty. She was glad of it.

When at last she felt warm enough, Melusina threw off the covering. It was softer than the girl's offering, but it, too, irritated her skin which was used to the smooth stroking of the sea.

Her legs were exposed and she stared at them. She had forgotten how ugly they were: slim and white and forked. She moved so that they were resting lightly on the floor. It felt so strange, a pressure on a flat surface. She had never before rested this way in her entire life. She glanced at the old man who watched her from a few feet away. He was still, but she sensed a restlessness beneath it, a watchfulness beyond his eyes. His entire body, she knew, would spring forward to help her if she faltered.

Well, she would not. He would see. The people of the sea were strong and hardy and far more than a match for the landfolk, who could not stay for more than a few moments under the ocean. She pressed her lips together and pushed herself off the bed.

For a moment she stood, her land legs locked firmly underneath her. Then, overbalanced, she fell forward and screamed.

The sound of it filled the shack, a piercing, wavering slide of sound. The old man leaped forward, agile despite his age, and caught her. He lowered her to the floor, but Melusina continued to scream.

The old man put his hands to his ears and screamed with her. "Lord help us," he cried out. "Stop it. It's a whale scream, it is. I haven't heard one since me whaling days. Stop it! You're tearing out me heart and ears."

He reached out to Melusina's shoulders and tried to stop her. But her screams went on and on. The old man began to shake her to get her to stop. His touch, his violence, silenced her, but he continued to shake her for long moments after she had ceased.

The violence in his hands reminded her of something. She could not think while he held her.

But finally, when he stopped, she knew. His hands were like Dylan's, the merrowman. She closed her eyes and could see them again as they beat against one another, accusing her, consigning her to the land.

She began to shake by herself then, and the old man touched her again, but this time with tenderness. He picked up her small hands in his.

"I know ye cannot understand me yet," he began.

Melusina opened her eyes and looked down at her hands in his. She wondered at his big, clumsy fingers that looked so naked without webbing. Then she looked up at his face and strained to understand. His mouth moved, but no bubble words came out, just peculiar scratchy noises. Was this how they talked then, these landfolk? Was this how she must talk now? She watched the old man's face for a clue.

"I know ye cannot understand me yet," the old man said. "Nor can I comprehend ye. But together . . ." and he dropped one of her hands and pointed first to himself and then to her. "Together, we will try. Yes?" He nodded and smiled. "Yes?"

The last sound he said several times. Melusina felt a great need to tell him she wanted to learn to talk with him. To say something in his language, in landtalk. She tried to imitate that short final sound: "*Eh. . . . eee . . . eh.*" She raised her chin as he did. "*Eh . . . eee . . . eh.*" It was not the same.

The old man grasped her chin in his rough hand. But his touch was still gentle. "Yes," he said, nodding and smiling.

She tried again. "*Eh . . . eee . . . eh.*" She opened her mouth like his.

"Oh, God," he said. "Oh, my dear God." He dropped his hands to his side. Then he collected himself and murmured, "The old tales were true. They were true. She's a fish gel for sure. In truth, in truth. She's got no tongue. No tongue at all."

Seven

It took Jess the better part of the next day to get over her sulks. She absolutely refused to talk to her mother, who tried signs and finger spelling as well as the exaggerated speech that she thought Jess understood so well.

Jess ignored her, pointedly taking off her hearing aid and leaving it within sight on the kitchen table.

If her anger had been directed at anyone but the captain, she would have run out of the house and down to the dock that stood in disrepair on their small private beach. She would have rowed out in her dinghy right to the captain's island and stayed there until dark, filling up her emptiness with the old man's stories and undemanding company.

But instead, Jess sat wrapped in resolute silence in the kitchen nook of the house, letting the early summer sun wash over her while she petted her blue-eyed white cat, Moby.

When the sun left the kitchen nook, traveling overhead toward the western side of the house, Jess decided she needed some fresh air. "It sorts things out. Clears the cobwebs from the head." She didn't realize it, but she was imitating the captain as she spoke. It was one of his favorite sayings.

She almost left her hearing aid on the table. "I only want to hear my own voice," she said to herself. " 'Cause I'm the only one who cares about me. So I'll only listen to me." She said it as belligerently as she could, under her breath. But in the end, she tucked the hearing aid carefully into her shirt pocket.

She walked down to the dinghy and, without thinking where she might row to, got in. She went out into the middle of the bay and decided to let the tide take her where it would. It took her to the island. Past a certain point in the bay, the incoming tide always landed her there.

As the boat scraped the rocky island beach, Jess got out. "Well, I *didn't* row here on purpose," she said, her chin jutting out defensively. "The boat brought me here on its own."

No one heard her but a gull, pecking pieces from some garbage washed up onto the beach. It cocked its head at the sound of her voice, but did not leave its meal.

Jess stomped off toward the dunes. She stopped suddenly, and dropped to her knees and crept the rest of the way to the top of the dune as if expecting an enemy to be lying in wait. When no one appeared, she went over the top. There was no one around. She got heavily to her feet and climbed the other dunes. When she saw the captain's shack before her, with its background of pine, she stopped a minute to look at it. Then, with a push from a sea breeze, she swooped down.

"Captain A. Captain A.," she called. "I'm here."

Without her hearing aid to guide her, she had no idea how loud she was. Nor did she hear the captain come around the side of the shack. All of a sudden, though, he was before her, grabbing her roughly by the arm.

"Hush ye, hush ye! I've gotten the tad to sleep at last."

But Jess, carried along by the momentum of her rush and by her great joy at seeing the old man, did not stop to try and read his lips. She just put her arms around his waist and hugged.

"Gentle, girl, gentle," he said to the top of her head and tried to disengage her arms.

Jess kept hugging and babbling about how much she had missed him and how glad she was to be back and could they go out for a row.

Finally, the captain sensed she was not hearing him at all. He pushed her away and spoke to her at arm's length, looking straight into her face. "The mermaid is asleep. She needs the rest. Let's be quiet and go up over the dunes and talk."

Straining at last to read his lips and watch his face, trying to catch any emotion from his mouth and eyes, Jess worked worry lines into her forehead. She could almost always read the captain's lips, just as she could puzzle out her mother's, especially if she had an idea of what they were going to say. Reading lips was an imperfect art, and it helped to know the people well. But she couldn't help being disappointed at the captain's greeting. It was all for the mermaid and none for her. Still, she was reluctant to let him go a second time, forgetting that it had been she who had run off. She took his hand and half pulled him up and over the dunes.

They found a sheltered place between two rises in the sand and sat there, Jess awkwardly and the old man carefully as if fearing a bone might splinter.

He reached over and took her hand in his, turning it over and over as if he had never looked at a young girl's hand before, then staring directly into her face and squinting a bit into the sun. "This mermaid," he said. "This miracle in my shack, we must be right grateful for having her. And careful, too."

Jess pulled her hand away. "She's just a girl. Like me."

"No, not like you, Jess. Not hardy and able to go where she pleases. She's new come to land, she is. She's lost all that she knows. She can't walk yet, humanlike." He hit his hand on his knees, bent down, then straightened up as if demonstrating something to Jess. "Scared she is. Homesick and scared and keening. And, Jess gel, she's got no one but us."

"She looks hardy enough to me," said Jess.

"Now, gel," the captain began.

But Jess was not to be stopped. "She's sulky and mean, and she threw my good sweater in the water for spite, and she's bewitched—yes, bewitched—

you and . . . and . . . and she didn't even say thank you."

"She's got no tongue." He said it blandly, his mouth barely moving, and it was so unexpected that Jess almost missed it completely.

"What?" In her puzzlement, she signed the question to him.

"She's got no tongue."

Jess was startled. "Oh. But how? I mean, was it an accident? Does it hurt? Are you sure?"

"It be natural, I expect," the old man said.

"Natural!"

"The old tales, some of 'em, said that the mermaids who got washed up on shore never learned to speak. There be one, I recollect, in old Holland. Got stuck in the mud. Some gels found her, took her home. Dressed her up in those Hollander clothes. Wooden shoes, too, I expect. Took to spinning with a right good skill. Never learned to speak." He shook his head at the memory of the story. "Never learned to speak."

Jess watched his lips carefully, taking it all in. She turned the story over and over in her mind the way the captain had examined her hand. She looked down at the sand and idly, without thinking, began drawing a mermaid with her finger. Long hair, long tail, webbed fingers, mouth open. She stopped and looked at the drawing. But no tongue. *No tongue.* It was horrible, having no tongue. The sound of it repeated in Jess's head. Being without good ears was bad enough. But what would a person do if she had no tongue? How would she speak? How could *any* mermaid speak?

"With her hands!" Jess shouted. "She talks with her hands. Like me. I can. We can. Together!"

The captain, who had been staring down at Jess's slowly evolving drawing, was startled by her outburst, for her excitement had completely overwhelmed her ability to speak clearly. And she had answered questions she had spoken only in her own mind. "What? What say ye?"

Jess slowed herself down. She had to be very clear. She had to make the captain understand completely. It was her plan. *Her* mermaid and *her* plan. Hands shaking, she took her hearing aid out of her pocket and put it on. Then she looked up at the captain and smiled.

"I can teach her to talk without a tongue. Me. With my fingers. Captain A., if I teach her finger spelling, she can tell us her name and . . . and about what it's like under the sea."

"But, gel, she can't *spell*. She doesn't know English," said the captain. "She knows Mermaid. And that b'ain't English, I'll warrant ye."

"Well, then . . . ," said Jess, but she was downcast. He was right. How could you possibly teach a mermaid English *and* finger spelling? It was too much.

"But you could teach her straight signs. Make up some, too, for words you don't know. Teach me, too. We'll all learn together. Just the three of us, gel. You and me and the tad." The three of them, just the three. It sounded so right. Just Jess and the captain and the girl from the sea. No one else. But, suddenly, Jess was not so certain. "Do you think I could? I mean, do you think she'd listen? Do you think she'd learn?"

The captain smiled and reached out to Jess. He took her hand again, swallowed it up in his, just like Jonah in the whale, as he always said. "I *know* you can. Why, if you can teach an old salt like me to finger-read and spell, slow and clumsy and full of the rheumatics as I be, you can teach a mermaid some signs. You can. You—Jess. To be sure."

"I can. I can. I know I can," Jess said. And her voice took on color and tone from her new-found dedication and joy.

Eight

Jess got up and hopped around excitedly. She was so full of her idea now, she could barely keep still. The captain rose, too, more slowly. But his face reflected Jess's happiness. He was very fond of her.

"*Now*, Captain A. Let's get her *now*. Let's teach her *now.*"

The old man started to shush her, but changed his mind. He followed her back to the shack, smiling as she capered over the dunes.

When they walked in, blinking a bit in the dark, the mermaid was already awake and sitting awkwardly up in the bed, clutching the blanket around her. She stared at them, no expression on her beautiful face.

Jess stopped and turned around to the captain. She whispered fiercely to him. "Are you sure she hasn't any tongue? Really sure?"

The old man didn't answer her. He walked over to the blanket-draped girl on the bed, picked her up, and carried her outside. As they walked into the light, she threw her arm up over her eyes, but otherwise did not move. He put her gently down and sat down by her in the sand. He put his hand to his back and winced, saying nothing.

Jess followed, almost reluctantly, and then sat above them on the dune. Little trickles of sand sped from her feet down to where they sat and eddied around them.

The captain smiled at the mergirl, but she did not return it, staring instead past the shack as if trying to scent out the sea.

"Over there, the sea is there," the old man said, gently turning her head around to face up and over the dune. "There." He pointed over the dune top. When she raised her chin and looked where he pointed, he nodded enthusiastically saying loudly, "Yes. Yes."

"*Eh . . . eee . . . eh.*" The mergirl tried to imitate him again, mouth open and straining.

From her perch, Jess could stare down into her mouth. It was a black hole. There was no tongue.

"Oh, no. You poor, poor thing. Oh, Captain A." Jess was suddenly in tears, and she leaped down next to the mergirl and grabbed her hands. The webbing between the mermaid's fingers was faint and dry and scaly. As Jess stared down at it, one of her tears dropped onto the webbing and where it touched, the skin sparkled and seemed, for an instant, to waver.

The mermaid looked down at her hand and then up to Jess's face. She took her hand away from Jess and brushed another tear right from under Jess's eye with her finger. Then she put the finger into her mouth, tasting the salt tear.

Her tongueless mouth dropped open, and she began to make a peculiar motion over and over with her hands. Hands on top of one another, right over left, dipped and dove. She touched the place where Jess's tear had been and then made the same motions. Again. And again.

"It's a word, Captain. I know it. A word. It must mean tear."

"It *be* a word, Jess. But I think it be more. It be too important a word to her. It be tear and salt water and . . ."

"Sea? Ocean? Captain A., it's her whole world."

"Tell her you understand, Jess gel. Let her know."

Jess touched her eye and made the same waving motion with her hand and pointed all around herself as if to a world filled with tears, with salt water. She made the sign over and over, and the mermaid made it back. Then the captain joined them.

"Captain, let's show her we *really* understand. We *can* talk." Jess was shouting now in her peculiar monotone, thick and full of emotion, against the wind. She grabbed the girl's hand and tried to pull her up, but the mermaid could not stand.

The old man bent over and struggled to his feet with the sea girl in his arms. He kept the blanket wrapped tightly around her, and this time she looked from side to side as they went over the dunes. In this way they came to the beach.

At the sight of the ocean, the mermaid stiffened and put her hand up over her eyes again. But when the captain sat down at water's edge with Jess next to them, Jess gently took the mermaid's hands from her eyes.

The tide lapped their feet as Jess spoke softly. "Look," she said, "water." And she made the mermaid's sign. Then she dipped her hands into the water and, without flicking the droplets from her fingers, made the sign again.

At that the girl looked at Jess and gave a half smile.

Jess grinned back. "We understand," she shouted. Then she quieted and said, "I'm Jess." Pointing to herself and giving the finger spelling for her name, she said "Jess. J-e-s-s."

The mergirl nodded. She seemed to understand. "Eh . . . eee . . . eh." Her chin lifted as she strained to speak.

Jess turned to the captain. "Is that *yes* or *Jess?*"

The old man shrugged. "Perhaps to her, now, they are the same."

Jess nodded solemnly. "They sound the same to me, too. I can't tell them apart. And in lip reading . . . well they look pretty much the same, too."

She looked directly at the mergirl again. "Jess," she said, pointing to herself again and signing.

This time the mermaid made the finger signs back, her fingers as fluid in the air as they must have been in water. When she finished, she turned to the captain and pointed at him.

"She wants my name, too," he said.

"Tell her."

"I forget how to do it."

"No, you don't. Remember, first the sign for

captain." She showed him, the curved fingers on the shoulder, like the epaulets of a uniform.

He did it quickly, smiling the whole time at Jess and the mermaid both.

"Then the finger-spelling A."

The sea girl picked up the two names quickly, signing them back again over and over.

"But what will we call you?" asked Jess, pointing to the girl.

Again she seemed to understand. She made a sign. It was the sea sign with a little flip with her thumb at the end, her right fist closed near her chin.

"Sea girl. She means sea girl," said Jess.

"Well, sea something anyway," said the captain.

"But it's our sign for girl. Look." She held her right hand in a fist, thumb up, along her chin line, then flattened it and, palm down, brought her hand away from her face, below the level of her cheek.

"I wonder . . . ," said the captain.

"What?" asked Jess, not really interested. She was repeating the mergirl's signs back to her, winning another half smile as her reward.

"I wonder," said Captain A. again to himself as he watched the two girls teaching each other to talk. "If we b'ain't all from the same place once upon a time. All spoke the same way, once upon a time. From land or from sea."

Nine

"Words," thought Melusina two days later, practicing the ones she had learned. She sat, alone, near the captain's shack. "Words are such slippery little things. Like bright little fish. Sometimes you can touch them, hold them, tell them what to do. But sometimes . . . ." She rolled over in the sand onto her back, pushing mightily with her arms, and stared up at the sky.

She was glad to be alone. The old man had gone off somewhere, after leaving her on the dune by his dwelling. The girl—Jess—had not yet come back from beyond the sand, beyond the dark night. Alone, Melusina could pretend that she was back in the ocean, swimming, floating on her back with the blue bowl of sky arching over her.

She wriggled a little, as she would in the water, but the sand got down her clothes and made her itch unbearably.

Those clothes. Jess's clothes. They still felt strange. Even a day later, Melusina wanted to claw them away from her. They clung uncomfortably to the body. They kept the skin from breathing. They reminded her of her beautiful lost tail by emphasizing the definition of her legs. She hated the clothes. Mermaids never draped more than a few strands of pearls or a necklace of shells over themselves. Yet Captain A. and Jess—she practiced their names with her hands—insisted that she had to wear something. They seemed disturbed that she wanted nothing on. And, to be totally honest, she knew the covering kept the wind off her arms and the hated legs. Kept her warm.

Warm. It was something she never had to worry about in the ocean. Oh, you could catch a warm or cold stream and ride along it for a while. And down in the deeps it was chilly and dark. But the main ocean, where they lived, rarely varied in temperature. She had never felt too warm or too cold in the sea.

She thought about the leg coverings, the pants. Though they emphasized her legs, they hid them, too, those strange, white, uncooperative limbs. She tried the word Jess had taught her again. Pants. Putting her palms against her body and drawing them slowly up to her waist. The pants did something else. It hid the place where her body and tail used to join. She shuddered and touched her waist once more, and this time put her right hand slowly into the top of the trousers and felt along her body. It was smooth. There was no longer the wonderful ridge where scales and hips met, the ridge whose definition grew more pronounced as mergirl became mermaid, mermaid became merwoman. There was nothing there now.

Just unbroken skin as smooth and unvaried as—as the sand. She drew her hand out and glanced at the webbing between her fingers. The webbing was brittle-looking and shrunken, but at least it was still there.

She pushed herself up into a sitting position and stared at her legs, at her toes. Little stubby fingers at the end of her body. She wiggled them slightly, first the big one, then the others. If they weren't so ugly, she could almost laugh at them. If they belonged to someone else, she would definitely laugh. Melusina thought about Jess's feet. At first she had wondered that the other girl had no toes. In their first learning time she had asked about that and been embarrassed—and frightened—when Jess had seemed to take off her foot. Slipped right out of it to reveal toes. The foot covering was called *shoe*. Jess made the word with her fingers. Imagine! Landfolk also covered their feet.

Jess had tried the shoes on Melusina, but they were too big and made her feet too hot. Besides, Melusina could not even feel the sand beneath her. The shoes disconnected her entirely from the world.

"In the sea we need no such coverings," Melusina said to herself, the words forming in little bubble pictures in her mind. But thinking about the sea made her long again for the touch of water on her body, and that made her remember that the only way to get there now was on her legs. She slapped her right leg with her hand. The sudden touch made a loud sound and a sting. Involuntarily she shook her leg at the blow, and then wondered at her lack of control. With her tail, she had always been able to go where she wanted. Perhaps, then, if she learned to control the legs, they would take her anywhere, too!

She didn't as yet know the word for moving-on-legs. It was something she would have to ask the landgirl or the old man when she saw them. But before Jess came back, Melusina promised herself she would learn to move-on-legs alone.

She closed her eyes from the brightness of the day, remembering how the captain and Jess had moved. Not flowingly like a mermaid, but with a peculiar rocking motion. One-two, one-two. She could recall the old man's rhythm as he carried her. She remembered the way Jess capered about by the edge of the sea.

Slowly Melusina bent her legs to the side, almost as if she still had a tail. She could not think one-leg-then-the-other. She still thought of her lower body as one piece. But if she could get up on her—whatever those bony protrusions in the middle of the leg were called—perhaps she could start. Her tail had bones. One could stand upon it, kneel upon it; perhaps one could do that with legs, too. So she would try to get upon the *kneel* part and go from there. At least, if she fell over, it would not be too far.

She pushed herself up, flailing her arms to keep her balance, but stayed on her *kneel*. The bony part of the legs tingled at first, but they did not hurt. It was as if they had been made for this.

She gave a quick little dolphin click back in her throat for joy. Next she would climb, using her hands. She looked around. It was all sand. There was nowhere to hold on and pull herself along. At each handhold, the sand would slip away from her.

She sank back onto her feet in a kind of sitting position and thought. "If I were in the sea . . ." the bubble thoughts popped and burst in her head. "If I were in the sea, I could swim over to a place where I could pull myself up."

Could one swim in the sand? Certainly not the same way as in the sea, arms by her side or thumbs linked together above her head. Instead, she would have to use her arms to pull herself along, and then up and over the dunes.

It was slow, so slow, and exhausting. Often, instead of pulling herself up, her hand would claw the sand down on top of her. But, at last, she reached the crest of the first dune. She gave a quick gasp and then rolled down the other side. The momentum carried her a small way up the next dune, but before she could take advantage of it, she had rolled back.

On her second up-dune climb, she tried to use her useless legs. When she tried to make them move together, like a tail, one sinuous movement, it didn't work. But when she relaxed and concentrated on her hands, the legs seemed to work on their own. Not together, but one at a time. Not right hand and foot together, but opposite hand and leg. She might not be able to manage moving on her feet, but on her *kneels*, moving like some great lumbering land turtle, and breathing heavily, for she was very tired, she made it to the top of the second dune and was rewarded with a sight of the sea.

"Great Lir," she thought, "give me strength now. Help me now." And she scrambled down the side of the dune, at first on her hands and the bony, rounded middle of the leg. Then her hands slipped out from beneath her, and she slid the rest of the way, her face in the sand. When she reached the bottom, she sat trembling and spat out a mouthful of sand. She could have cried; she wanted to. But pride kept her from it. And she was only two dunes from the beach. She had counted them when she had been granted that sight of the sea.

The next dunes were smaller, gentler, and she got up and down them more easily, having perfected a sideward roll with her arms held above her as if in a dive. And so she came at last, feeling gritty and sandy but filled with real pride, to the slightly damp beach. She could feel the memory of the last tide below her hands. Crawling slowly, carefully, with only one bad scrape on her *kneel* from a shell she had not noticed, she made it to the edge of the ocean.

She held out her hands before her and shaped her relief at the sea. She knew no one was watching; still she fairly ached to call to someone, merfolk or landfolk. She wanted to say that she— Melusina—had come by herself on her land legs to the sea.

She laughed and flung her arms to the sky and

gave the call of the great whale when it sang to its
mate of the open seas, of dangers past, of great
dives to come.

Then quietly, calmly, she crept hand over hand,
kneel over *kneel*, into the waiting water.

Ten

It took nearly two weeks before Melusina could tell them anything about herself. She had many words by then: Jess, Captain A., ocean, sand, boat, house, shell, girl, man, the parts of the body, and all the most important verbs. She could even tell them how she felt: happy, sad, lonely, quiet, hungry, sleepy, curious. And she had finally mastered the awful legs, so stiff and separate and complex.

But all the details of her story, how she came to be on that beach at that time, were impossible to relate. She was not even sure how much she dared tell. If she had been punished for being *seen*, what could the punishment be for *telling*? So she settled for an abbreviated version which, with finger signs and some pantomiming, was all she could or would manage.

They were all three sitting on the beach near the water, Melusina's special place. A light breeze was blowing and the salt smell, the nearness of the ocean, made her throat ache with remembering. It made her ache in a way that swimming did not. When she was swimming even though her eyes smarted and the water still felt strange as it slipped between her legs, and she could not stay under for more than a minute, she could still pretend she was back with her own kind.

Melusina looked at her two companions, the old man and the girl. She wanted so much to tell them, to make them understand, to see as she did, the shimmering underwater world with the rays of light filtering through and touching the fish and the plants with a wand of bright color. See as she did the schools of merfolk busy at their chores, farming the sea bottom, salvaging treasures from the old wrecks. Hear, as she did, the soft murmurations of ocean life, the songs of whales, and the dolphins' chatter, the bubbling recitation of the seafolk's sagas. Why she, herself, could bubble-name her mermothers back a hundred generations and Dylan, though she grimaced at the thought of him, knew all the stories from the Irish coast—and told them all well.

But there was no way to tell Jess and the captain everything. Perhaps it was just as well. For if they knew, really knew, wouldn't they tell? Were they to be trusted more than anyone else on land? Melusina didn't know. So she began her story in its shortest form.

With her hands, she said, "I was seen swimming by a landperson. I was with the turtle. And the fish. I jumped. There was a boat. There was a girl. A girl with hair, so." She sketched braids on either side of her own head. Then suddenly she looked at Jess and for the first time made the connection:

"*You!*" It had been Jess. It was Jess's fault that she was here. Jess's fault that she was *seen*. If Jess should not have *seen* her, then surely Jess should not know the story at all. But now she had told her. Would there be more punishment? Would it be worse? What could be worse than this? With a wild, inarticulate cry, she threw herself down on the beach and sobbed loudly, like a girl from the land.

Jess and the captain looked at one another. They did not understand the mermaid's moods. She was as changeable as the tides. One minute she was ecstatic, capering over the dunes in Jess's outgrown cutoffs and shirt, the next face down near the water's edge, her body shuddering with its wild sobs.

"What did she mean *this* time?" asked Jess.

The old man chewed on the stem of his pipe which he rarely lit. "She seems to have recognized you."

"You mean when I saw her jump up? From the boat?"

"When you *saw* her."

"Is that what she means by *seen*. Why the word *seen* is so important?"

The captain nodded.

"Well, what's wrong with being seen? I see you, you see me. We see each other. Sounds like a lesson from school. I'd rather be seen than heard!" Jess spoke almost angrily and pushed her foot into the sand, burying it up to the arch.

"Depends what school you're in," said the captain.

"What does that mean?" said Jess. "What school?" She paused; then her face took on a sly look. "Like a school of fish?"

The captain still did not answer, staring at the sobbing sea girl.

"I said *like a school of fish*!" As always, when she was excited, Jess's voice got thicker and harder to understand.

The captain knocked his pipe on the beach absently and still said nothing.

Jess was ready to scream at the old man when he finally looked directly at her and nodded. So, instead, in a quiet voice, she said, "If you're in a school of merpeople . . ."

"Merfolk, they calls it."

"*Merfolk*. You shouldn't be seen."

The captain nodded again. "Why not, gel?" He said it as much to himself as to Jess.

"Because . . . because . . . because then landfolk would know you exist."

"And . . . ," the old man prompted.

Jess thought this over carefully before she answered. "And they'd hunt you and put you in aquariums and zoos and study you and . . . ." She shuddered.

"And . . . ," the captain prompted again, but Jess looked pale under her tan. She couldn't go on.

"And," she said at last in a very small voice, "maybe mermaid tails are . . . good to eat. Or something."

The old man looked grim. "Or something. I wouldn't be surprised. I'm never surprised at what *landfolk* do."

Jess stood up and put her hands on her hips. "Well, we can't tell anyone. It's settled."

The captain lifted up his cap and put his pipe behind his ear. He flattened his shreds of white hair down over his scalp and replaced the cap. "Looking at her now," he said, "who would believe us anyway?"

Jess looked at the mermaid stretched out in the sand. Her legs were now tanned, and, in her cutoffs and shirt, she looked like any landgirl, having a tantrum. Jess smiled a quick, toothy grin. Then she looked serious again. "But of course. That's why they did it."

"Did what?"

"Made her into one of us. Turned her like that. They. The ones who didn't want her seen."

Captain A. nodded. "Tell her Jess. Tell her we understand."

Jess walked over to the mermaid, who had stopped sobbing at last and was lying still. She touched Melusina on the shoulder and turned her over. Then, hands on her friend's shoulder, she began to tell her just that.

Eleven

The girls were together every day after that. The summer sun turned them both brown, and Melusina's legs grew firm and strong from the walking and running she did. The old man, happy to see the two girls happy and tired by their chattering hands and energy, often left them alone, staying in his shack or going off all day in his boat while the two of them played on the beach and in the waters of the island's cove.

It had taken a little while for Melusina to be persuaded to ride in Jess's dinghy. Her memories of boats were all negative ones. Boats meant people—and being seen. But after the first time out, the motion of the waves and the sight of land far off were so appealing to Melusina that she insisted they ride in the dinghy as often as possible. Jess did not realize it, but Melusina would sit in the boat and pretend she was home.

It was from the boat that they first saw the great turtle together. Jess was so excited, she nearly fell out of the dinghy, for the turtle came alongside and bumped the boat with his shell.

Jess turned to Melusina, who was sitting in the bow, high up, eyes closed, hair blowing.

"Melusina," Jess called, for the sea girl now knew the sound of her own name. "Look."

Melusina shook herself as if shaking off a dream and turned around and followed Jess's pointing finger. Jess called out and signed. "Look. I recognize him. I've seen him before. See the scars on his back."

But Melusina did not stop to try and read Jess's fingers. She stood up, let out a strange sound that was piercing, high, and sweet. Then she took two steps, stumbling a bit, into the middle of the dinghy, nearly turning them over.

"Sit down. Sit down," screamed Jess, forgetting to sign with her hands. She was too busy trying to right the boat. "Sit down. What are you doing?"

But Melusina was already down, and leaning half out of the boat. Her hands lovingly cupped the turtle's head. Then she beat a short tattoo on the turtle's shell and waved as he sank back to resurface again a yard off their port side.

Jess was still trying to steady the boat when Melusina turned to her, held out her hands, and smiled. It was the first true smile she had ever given Jess, and her teeth showed pearly white in the sun.

"Grandfather," she signed with her fingers and pointed to the turtle who was swimming leisurely away from them.

"Oh, come on," said Jess. "How can a turtle be your grandfather?"

But Melusina smiled again and said the word over, and though Jess pressed her, she would give no further explanation. So Jess took Grandfather to be the turtle's name.

After that, Grandfather surfaced regularly when they took the dinghy out. Indeed, Jess was half certain Melusina took the dinghy into the cove just to see the old turtle perform. He would swim around and around while Jess applauded and Melusina's fingers flickered under the waves like bright little sea creatures. She always bent over the boat and put her hands in the waves and said she talked to him.

Half of Jess felt glad when Melusina talked to Grandfather, because the mermaid became animated and happy. But the other half of Jess was painfully jealous. It was the same feeling she got when she saw the children at school laughing and chattering together, quietly, effortlessly. Jealous— and left out.

Once Melusina even bent over and put her face into the water, causing a profusion of bubbles to rise, bursting and popping so furiously that Jess became frightened and tried to pull her up. The two girls struggled briefly, and then Melusina lifted her head out of the water, coughed, spit, shook her head, and made a high keening sound.

When Melusina was calm again, and the turtle had disappeared back into the deep, she turned to Jess and tried to explain with hand signs and miming.

"Sometimes I forget I can no longer breathe in

the water, But I want so to talk to him."

"Him?"

"Grandfather."

"But you talk with your fingers," said Jess.

"Bubbles, mouth talk, is better."

"Bubbles? Mouth talk?" Jess was astonished. It had never occurred to her that the tongueless Melusina could talk other than with her hands.

Melusina nodded vigorously.

"Could you . . . could you teach me?" Jess asked.

"Could you . . . could you learn?" Melusina answered with her fingers, watching Jess closely with both a teasing shyness and a concern.

"If I want to, I can learn anything," said Jess a bit boastfully, but she suddenly felt she could.

So Jess rowed them ashore. And on the turning of the tide, they both waded far out into the water. Jess was in her bathing suit, and Melusina, as always, insisted on going into the water wearing nothing at all. Jess was always afraid that someone might see them, though no one but the captain ever came to his island. Jess was half repelled, half fascinated by Melusina's body, so like and yet unlike her own. For Melusina was smaller than Jess but seemed years older, with bubble jewels of breasts. Her body was eel-slim, hipless, hairless, and strangest of all, she had no navel. Didn't, in fact, know what a navel was for. When Melusina and Jess turned after a frustrating discussion about such things once, the captain had shrugged and said: "Maybe she be born in an egg. Like some fish." It was his last word on the matter.

Jess followed Melusina into the shallows. They found a pocket where they could sit on the bottom, chin deep in the water, yet not be disturbed by the gently ebbing tide. Melusina put her face in the water, and Jess did the same. As Jess watched underwater, Melusina blew bubbles from her mouth and nose, bubbles that seemed to have a life of their own, twisting and traveling in different directions. Some were small, round jewels. Some were great, globby oval masses. Melusina suddenly withdrew her face, and Jess did, too.

In finger signs, she spoke to Jess. "Watch carefully. I will now say in bubble talk, 'I like you, friend.' " Then she put her head under again.

Jess hastily put her face in, too. As she watched, three gentle well-shaped bubbles detached themselves from Melusina's mouth. The first caressed her right cheek, while the second seemed to hesitate and sink for a moment to chest level, then rise. And the third bubble floated toward Jess's nose, stopped still for a moment, then popped and floated to the top in millions of tiny circles, except for one that touched Jess's lip and refused to leave. She finally had to blow it away from her, and it lifted lazily to the silvery ceiling of the sea.

Jess followed the bubble to the top with her eyes, then followed its motion with her head and lifted her head out of the water. She shook herself vigorously, splattering them both. "How did you

do that?" she asked. Then, remembering Melusina couldn't read her lips, she hastened to form a question mark with her finger in the air.

Melusina wiggled closer to her and opened her mouth. She made a hollow cave with it and then pursed her lips. She seemed to fill her mouth with air and then blow out. There was such force to her breath that Jess staggered back a bit.

"Hey, cut it out," she cried.

Melusina laughed, a silent laugh. She pointed to Jess and signed, "You try."

Jess filled her mouth with air and blew. It was weak in comparison.

Melusina pushed her wet hair behind her ears and then signed, "In the water."

Obediently Jess put her face down. Her braids floated out behind her. She blew some quick bubbles and, by accident, snorted in some water. She raised her head and coughed. Her eyes burned and her nose dripped.

When at last she had cleared her throat and nose, she looked over at Melusina who was shaking her head.

"Well, did I say anything? What did I say?" Jess asked. "Under the water. What did I say?"

Melusina covered her mouth with her webbed hands. She rolled her eyes. Then she removed her hands and smiled. With her fingers she said, "You said *Help! Water! Need air!*" And at each word, Melusina punctuated it with her strange silent laugh.

"Oh, I did not," said Jess angrily. "Now be fair. I taught you. Now you teach me."

At that, Melusina took Jess's hand and dragged her up, leading her to the shore. Then she sat down again, at the water's edge and pulled Jess down with her. She took Jess's face in her hands, and Jess felt again how cool, even clammy, Melusina's smooth skin was.

Melusina touched Jess's mouth and then pointed to her own. She opened it again, and again Jess saw how like a deep wound it was, empty, tongue-less.

Melusina put her hand by the side of her mouth and wiggled her index finger. "This," she said, meaning tongue, "is wrong. Not good. Cannot speak with this in water."

"Never?" signed Jess, palm down and slowly.

Melusina looked away. Then just as carefully and with pains, for she understood Jess's desire to be able to speak in the sea as she could not on land, Melusina signed: "I cannot speak with my mouth on land. You cannot speak with your mouth in water. We must speak together, on land and in sea, hand on hand, as friends do. Hand on hand. Forever."

She held out her hand then to Jess.

Jess reached out and touched the mermaid's cold fingers and brought them up to her own warm cheek. "Forever," she signed with the other hand in that circle that sealed each of them in.

Twelve

The next evening, the girls were alone on the island beach. Captain A. had gone to town on his once-a-month trip. He would buy his provisions, visit old friends, drinking and smoking and telling tales far into the night. Then he would sleep late into the next day and come home on the afternoon tide.

The girls had planned an overnight together at the shack. With a few misstatements, not exactly lies, Jess had led her mother to believe that Melusina was in some way related to the old man. She feared to give away the mermaid's secret, though later she realized she would not have been believed even if she had tried.

"You have a friend!" her mother said with great enthusiasm. "Who is it? Where does she live? What kind of girl is she? What does her father do?" And seeing Jess's mouth tighten and reading it as misunderstanding, her mother slowed down the questions and tried to enunciate them with great care.

But Jess had understood. Reading her mother's lips was rarely a problem. The problem was the questions themselves. The secret, Melusina's secret, had to be maintained. So Jess timed her answers to be exasperatingly slow and to break in over her mother's voice as if she did not hear her at all.

"Her name is Melusina. She has no father. Like me. Her mother lives—far away. She is visiting Captain A. And I'll need my sleeping bag and toothbrush."

And so the permission had been won, and Jess had escaped with the sleeping bag, toothbrush, and a box of brownies as well. She added it to the table where the girls set about making dinner for themselves. It was to be vegetarian fare, for Melusina steadfastly refused to eat meat or fish. And the captain, grudgingly, had changed his diet for her. Jess suspected that once ashore, he was going to indulge himself in lobster and shrimp.

"From my mother," she said, opening the plastic box containing the brownies. She rarely mentioned her home life at all to Melusina. The other girl nodded at the signs.

"What's *your* mother like?" asked Jess suddenly. "Is she like mine—meaning well but full of questions?" She made a series of little question marks in the air between them.

Melusina looked at her strangely. "Why do you make fun of your mother? Don't you like her?"

"I guess I like her. But I don't like all her questions." Jess shrugged. "And I don't like her hovering over me all the time."

"Hovering?"

"She worries because of my deafness, my ears. She blames herself for them. And she blames me because of her divorce. She doesn't really say anything out loud. But I can tell. So instead, she is too nice, and too sweet, and too . . . too hovering."

The mergirl shook her head. "I don't understand. How is she to blame for your ears? And how are you to blame for . . . for that other?"

Fingers flying, Jess tried to explain. She showed Melusina with her hands how she had grown inside her mother until, at a crucial time, her mother had gotten sick, and the disease had carried itself over to the baby who was developing inside. The disease had affected the unborn baby's ears. When she had been born, the burden of a deaf child had been too much for her father. He had left them both, never seen them again. Jess worked hard with fingers and miming to tell the story, but it was an impossible task. Melusina knew nothing of wombs and babies and divorce. She looked positively ill when Jess talked about the disease and growing inside her mother. And there the story got stuck.

At last Jess said in desperation, "Never mind *my* mother. Tell me about *yours*."

Melusina stopped, hands in midair with a question. She opened her mouth and closed it. She twitched her fingers for a second, then as if forcing them to be quiet, made them still. At last her hands spoke. "I cannot."

"Why not?"

Melusina shook her head.

"Are you afraid I will tell?"

Melusina shrugged almost imperceptibly, but did not answer, so Jess went on.

"Even if I would tell, which I won't, I wouldn't be believed. Landfolk wouldn't believe about mer-folk. They don't want to believe, and so they don't." Jess watched the words spill from her own fingers. Even to her, the explanation looked flat.

"*You* believe."

"That's because I saw you. And yet . . . yet . . ." Jess shrugged, too. Then she looked up at Melusina's face and smiled.

Melusina gave her a smile in return.

Jess said again, certain this time of success, "Tell me about your mother. One friend to another."

Melusina sat down at the table and began. As she spoke, her fingers flowed and swam through the air. Even when they stumbled over a word, she made a world of such beauty and peace that Jess nearly wept to hear of it. She saw and felt the sea moving around them, and saw and felt the bright flashes of underwater color and the soft caressing of the tide. Jess understood Melusina's world, a world in which everything touched, everything belonged.

"And my mother sings to me," Melusina continued. "She tells me poems."

"*Sings* to you?" Jess made a face. "How could she sing to you. How could she tell you poems? You don't have any . . ." She stopped herself just in time, but the word *tongue* hung between them, unsigned in the air. Jess felt ashamed of her unthinking cruelty.

Melusina looked over the table past Jess for a long time. Then she focused on the landgirl at last. "My mother can sing two kinds of songs," she said. "The great whale songs and the songs with words that she sings with her hands. Haven't you ever heard the songs that hands can sing or the poems that fingers can tell?"

Jess looked bewildered. "I . . . I'm not sure," she said. "I only had two years in the special school. And I never liked to talk much with my hands. It always seemed too . . . too . . . revealing, I guess. It let everyone know I was—impaired."

Melusina glanced down at her hands. She wiggled the fingers experimentally. "I'm not sure if I can explain," she said. Her fingers stuttered a moment. "But . . . but . . . perhaps."

"Please," said Jess. It held all the longing she had never let out before.

"Well, say this," instructed Melusina. Quickly she made the familiar signs for *The mermaid dove into the sea*: thumb along the chin for girl, the waving hands for fish, the diving motion with the hands going toward the floor, the sign for "into," and the sign for "sea."

Jess, puzzled, repeated the signs, first one at a time, then with her usual fluid succession.

Melusina nodded, not smiling. "But, if you say it like this, it is a poem." She said, *"The mermaid dove into the sea,"* but it was different this time. As she brought her finger along her chin for girl, she let her fingers swim, fishlike, below the thumb. It caused her thumb to waver a bit, too. She managed to get that wavering, swimming motion into the other signs as well.

Jess tried signing that way.

Melusina joined her, and they tried it three times together.

"It *is* a poem," said Jess. Instead of saying simply *The mermaid dove into the sea*, what she said was more like *The fish girl dove fishlike into the fish-filled sea*. But it was more than that. The whole sentence was now filled with the feeling of waves and waviness, of joyful diving and the motion of the sea. The line spun off her fingers that way had a rhythm of its own and a melody as well. It was a poem *and* a song.

Jess signed it again, first word by word the old way. Then she said it as a poem. The difference was so great, her mouth dropped open and a sob tore out of her. She looked over at Melusina, and Melusina was grinning broadly.

"That's beautiful," Jess said aloud. But then realizing that Melusina had not understood her spoken words, she realized something else as well. "It's gone. Your world is gone for you. Why did you have to leave it? Why?" She signed the questions.

Melusina looked down at her own fingers then. She spread them wide which pulled the webbings white between them. She seemed to be deep in thought.

Suddenly she looked up and signed. "The Three Wisdoms is the creed we live by." She had some trouble with the word *creed*, but Jess instinctively knew what she meant. "It is what we learn first when we are tads, when we are still unschooled. It is to protect us, each one individually, and the People as a whole. But I never understood them till I came to the shore."

Jess held her breath. She wanted to ask what the Three Wisdoms were, but she feared to break in.

"And the Wisdoms are these. Have patience, like the sea. Move with the rhythm of life around you. Know that all things touch all others, as all life touches and is touched by the sea. The last, I think, is the most important, though no one ever told me so." She finished with a flourish and was silent then. Her mouth moved, lips working against one another, as if following her own thoughts.

Jess leaned across the table and touched Melusina's hand. "We say something a little like that, too. On land. It's our creed, too. Only we call it the golden rule."

"Why *golden*?" asked Melusina.

"I guess because gold is supposed to be the most precious thing in the world."

Melusina shook her head. "In the sea we say, 'As *precious as a mermaid's tear*.' "

They both smiled then, remembering how Melusina had already shed one in the captain's shack. Then Jess, suddenly uncomfortable with all the talk and tired from signing, pointed to the plate of vegetables. "Come on," she said, her hand pointing from the plate to her mouth in hasty motions. "Let's eat."

Thirteen

They ate and cleaned up, then made the shack shipshape the way the captain had shown them. With the summer sun still two hours before setting, they planned to swim and watch the sunset before coming back inside to sleep.

Melusina felt as if she had been scrubbed clean of emotions. She had held back so long, held back about the world under the waves, about her mother and the merfolk, and about the terrible righteousness of Dylan's anger. But while they ate, she told Jess all. And as she explained, it had come to her, for the first time, what the Wisdoms were all about and how, playfully, she had ignored them, violated them. She wondered if there would ever be a time that she could tell her mother, tell Lir, even tell Dylan, that she understood at last. She wondered if there would ever be a time she could prove to them that she had changed.

Changed. Surely she had. She looked down at her legs, now as much a part of her as the tail had once been. Yes, anyone with eyes could see she was changed. Outside. But how could anyone ever know how changed she was inside, too? Well, it did not matter. Life on the land was what mattered now. She would have to make of it what she could.

Glancing over at Jess in the cabin's flickering candlelight, Melusina thought about how hard it was for the landgirl to speak. Like Melusina herself, Jess walked with a great burden. But Jess's had been a burden since birth. She remembered Jess's first movements toward her, quick and angry. The landgirl had rarely smiled. Yet lately, especially tonight, there had been a softness, a caring, many smiles. Perhaps, Melusina thought to herself, Jess had needed to know about the Three Wisdoms. True, they were wisdoms of the sea—but they could mean as much on the land. Perhaps Melusina had been meant to come from the sea just to share the Wisdoms. "Oh, Great Lir," Melusina signed in her own language, "if that is so, then I think I can bear this exile."

She shook her head slightly at her thoughts and got a rough towel from the shelf. It was for Jess, not herself. She still preferred to be dried by the wind. She handed it to the landgirl, who took it with a smile.

They marched together to the beach.

Melusina always thought the swimming was especially good in the evenings. There was a quietness, a stillness in the air. No great ships moved out of the harbor, crossing the horizon at dusk. Even though the island was away from the big port town, it still disturbed her to see so many boats. Only at night did she truly feel safe.

She got out of her clothes and ran into the water. It molded itself to her like a second skin. As long as she did not have to lose this water world entirely to gain the land, she could almost be content. She dove under the waves and felt her long unbound hair string out behind.

Later the two of them sat on the beach side by side. Jess sat on the big towel, dabbing herself with a smaller one. But Melusina sat directly on the sand and was dried by the wind off the sea.

They were quiet then, not jabbering with fingers for a change. Melusina closed her eyes and tried to feel the contours of the land beneath her.

"Look. Melusina, look."

The fear in the voice caused her to open her eyes at once, and she followed Jess's pointing finger. There was something flashing gray and then black tumbling in on the tide. Melusina could not make it out, her eyes weaker in the air than in the sea. But it was Jess who told her.

"Dolphin," she cried.

And at that moment, the dolphin spoke to her, called, in its high whistling click. It was sick, it was failing, it was being carried by the strong undertow slowly onto the sand.

Melusina was frantic. She turned to Jess and spoke quickly with her hands. If it was beached, there was no way the two of them could get it off the island again. A dolphin, even a small one, would outweigh them both by two or three times. And once the tide ebbed, the dolphin would be left there for good, to dry up and die, to rot, its laughing face eaten by the garbage pickers of the sea, the gulls.

She lifted her head and called back to it. Dolphin talk was a peculiar blend of whistles, clicks, and barks. But it was simple. She had learned it first of all the water languages, even before she had known bubble talk. She called to it. "Turn. Danger. Go. Danger. Not come. Go. Danger. Danger."

Her cry was sharp and sad. The dolphin heard her, but its answer was weak. "No turn. Sick. No turn. Come. Help. Come."

Melusina grabbed Jess's hand and tried to get her to go into the sea, for their only hope was to turn the dolphin when it was still in the water.

But they were too late. They were ankle-deep when the dolphin was washed ashore at their feet, its beaklike snout trying to raise the rest of its bulk out of the water. It looked up at Melusina for an instant, chattered, "Sick. Help." Then its head flopped back onto the sand. The tide rushed in around it.

Melusina splashed into the shallow water by its side. She put a hand on its back and moaned.

The dolphin's black eye moved to see her, seemed to recognize something about her, and blinked. She patted it with a swift tattoo of her hands and ran her fingers over its still wet, sparkling skin. The smooth side was so familiar to her touch. She put her head on its back and was very still.

A sound above her caused her to look up. It was Jess, fingers flying. "A dolphin. I was right."

Melusina nodded, continuing to stroke its head.

"Won't it die if we can't get it back to the sea?"

Melusina nodded again, and patted out a com-forting rhythm on the dolphin's side. It blinked at her once more and gave a high whistling sigh.

"What can we do?"

Do? Melusina knew there was nothing the two of them could do, small and weak as they were. The dolphin was not even full grown, still a calf. Perhaps it had been rammed and injured by a boat and in its weakened state, caught by the undertow. But even though it was a small dolphin, it was too big for them. What *could* they do but comfort it and hope the tide could somehow take it away at flood.

Before she could sign these thoughts to Jess, the other girl had run across the dunes and disappeared in the direction of the shack. Melusina watched her go. Was she not going to help? Would she not sit by the dolphin and help her keep it in touch with life?

She looked back at the dolphin. It was already beginning to dry out. Its dark skin in the setting sun reflected a dull pink. There were sprinkles of silver where wet droplets still flecked its sides. As long as the tide was in, it would live. But when the tide turned, went out, when the morning sun came, how much time would it have then?

Melusina stood up and walked around the front of the dolphin, never letting her touch stray from its skin. All life touches the sea. This she knew. And creatures of the sea valued the mermaid's touch. Some of them even believed it cured. She only wished she could cure this poor child of the sea.

As she rounded the dolphin's beaked snout, she looked out at the sea and saw her old friend the tortoise.

"Grandfather," she said to herself.

He raised his neck and one flipper to her, and she signed back with one hand. She called to him with the signs of the sea: "Help. Help for the ocean calf. Tell them, Grandfather. Tell them from me."

Then she turned back to the big sea child who breathed heavily, hopelessly, on the beach by her feet.

Fourteen

The tortoise had barely dived when Jess was back, dragging the lobster barrel behind her. She could not catch her breath and had to stop frequently as she came over the final dune. Yet Melusina did not leave the dolphin to help her.

"Come on. Over here," called Jess. She gestured with her hand.

But when Melusina did not stir from the sea creature's side, Jess dragged the barrel herself to the water's edge. Her breathing was almost as heavy as the dolphin's.

"We can keep the dolphin wet until the captain returns." She worked her fingers slowly.

"But it is wet enough, wet enough for the night," said Melusina with one hand. "I do not understand."

"You said it would dry out and die. You said it would rot and be eaten. You said . . ."

"But it will not dry out completely without the sun on its back."

Jess shook her head. "No? But how will it breathe? It needs the water."

"No, this one breathes air, even as you. And I."

· 94 ·

Jess looked down at the dolphin. "But . . ."

Melusina, still stroking the calf, said, "It was born as you were, from its mother. That I understand. It suckled at it's mother's breast. It breathes air. You really have more in common with it than I." She made a strange sound back in her throat, and it was a kind of laugh.

"Then what can we do for it?"

Melusina looked sorrowful. "Comfort it. Touch it. Let it know we care."

Jess did not go closer to the dolphin. "When the captain gets here, he can go for the Coast Guard." It had been part of the plan, her plan.

"Coast Guard?"

Jess hesitated, trying to find the right words. "Men who watch the seas and the shores. Who help." She made the signs carefully with her fingers.

"Coast Guard," Melusina repeated.

"They could tie a rope around its tail and tow it back. Or maybe three or four of them could pick it up and walk it back into the sea."

Melusina nodded. But she did not stop stroking the beast.

"Or I could go now myself and find them." But they both knew that it was but minutes before the beach would be totally black. It was too dangerous for Jess to be alone in her dinghy in the harbor at high tide without lights of any kind. And even if she made it, would the Coast Guard come at night for such a mission?

"I bet it does need water," said Jess. She looked

around helplessly at the barrel, now half floating in the incoming tide.

Melusina shook her head, and the two of them stopped talking, for in the dark they could no longer make out their hand signals. Occasionally the dolphin would click and Melusina would return its confidence. But except for that and the pounding of the sea, there was no sound at all.

After a few minutes, Jess leaped up. "I'll get us some food."

Since Melusina didn't understand her, Jess really called out for her own comfort. She had turned up her hearing aid, and still the silence seemed only to echo more silence. The occasional clicking chatter of the dolphin and Melusina made her feel lonely, left out. She needed to do something, take some action. If Melusina said the dolphin didn't need water, well perhaps she was right. Who would know better than a mermaid? But the need to do something, anything, drove Jess up and over the dunes in the dark.

A half-moon low in the sky gave her some faint light. It was dodging clouds, but came out in time for her to see the captain's shack below. She ran to the shack in a rush.

Inside, the candle lantern had burned low, but she could still see enough to gather a bag of vegetables, two cans of soda, the left-over brownies, and a flashlight.

She hurried back with the lantern and the food slung in her sleeping bag. She dumped them on the sand well out of the reach of the tide. Picking up the lantern, she went over to where Melusina knelt by the dolphin. It lay like some great sea monster. She was suddenly afraid of it.

In the flickering light, she could see Melusina's hands working at words. She brought the lantern up close so that she could read her friend's fingers.

"Come here. Come by me," Melusina's hands said. In the lantern light, they seemed disembodied, to be speaking by themselves.

Jess hesitated. Then slowly she walked around the back end of the dolphin and, ankle-deep in the seawater, stood by Melusina's side.

"Give me your hand," Melusina said. Jess could read it when she got close.

Almost shyly, Jess reached out her hand, and for the first time the sea girl threaded her own fingers through Jess's. The webbing seemed to pulse with a life of its own. Then Melusina withdrew her fingers and held up her hand to the light. She spoke slowly with the one hand.

"Everything needs to be touched. Life touches life. Calls to life. So the dolphin—her name is Wave Greeter—needs us now most of all. Put your hand on her. Let her feel your touch."

Jess shook her head. In the dark, the idea of putting her hand on a clammy dolphin was suddenly repellent.

"Please," signed Melusina, "Need is great." She moved her hand toward her body, the five fingers curved, to emphasize the need. Then she held out her hand to Jess. At that moment the cloud moved

away from the moon.

Jess could see the pleading in Melusina's face, could feel it between them. Nervously she put her own hand out to the mermaid. Melusina grasped it lightly and put it, palm down, on the dolphin's nose. The nose was a bit clammy, but more like a dog's wet from a swim.

At her touch, the dolphin seemed to breathe a whistling sigh, called out once in swift, high-pitched clicks, and was still.

Melusina released her hold on Jess's hand and signed to Jess. But Jess did not read the words. She closed her eyes and tried to send her own thoughts to the sea beast, Wave Greeter, who breathed just below her hand. "Hold fast, Wave Greeter. Jess says hold fast."

Fifteen

The girls sat, stood, knelt for hours by the dolphin, rarely speaking to one another except to nod. The pale, worn-out half of the moon traveled slowly across the night sky. The tide came in and came to full flood. The lantern burned out.

Jess, who had begun to shiver uncontrollably, signed at last, "I have to sleep, to get warm. Just a little while. Then I will come back. Then you can sleep."

Melusina nodded. "I will stay."

Jess got up on numbed, cramped legs and stumbled to the sleeping bag. She lay down and was instantly asleep, her face still turned toward the dolphin and her friend.

But Melusina waited. And while she waited, hand on the dolphin's side, speaking with her fingers into its skin, the tide turned. At its turning, Melusina felt the old stirring in her blood, for a mermaid's blood ebbs and flows to the rhythm of the tide.

"I am still of the sea," she thought to herself. "It will never leave me."

She threw her head back, her hair making black waves down her back, and she sang. It was high and sweet and clear, the wordless song of the whale for the sea. And as she sang and the tide turned, the merfolk came up out of the sea, riding the crests of the waves. Lir was in the front, and the rest of the pod fanned out behind him in a shimmering formation like a great trident. The light from the old moon cast their faces in silver. Behind Lir and to his right, Melusina could see her mother. The look of sorrow intermixed with joy on her face confused Melusina. She did not speak, could not speak. She knew they came for the dolphin and not for her. And for their care and their speed in coming, she was thankful and felt blessed, indeed, just to see them again.

Carefully she stepped away from Wave Greeter, so that it was clear she asked nothing for herself. She put her hands above her head and said as formally as possible, "We have kept by her all night, my friend and I. I give the *tad* to your care."

She had been going to say simply "calf," but at the last minute she had substituted the word *tad* because it had been Lir's word for her and she wanted, somehow, to show him a kind of late gratitude and understanding. But the word itself, as she spoke it into the night, seemed to cause him pain instead. His great silvered face creased, and an agony passed over his features. She would have cut off her hand for the hurt she gave him.

He did not speak, nor did any of them. But

Melusina did not find that strange. She was now of the land, and it was even a violation that they had allowed themselves to be *seen* by her. They would never try to speak.

She checked quickly over her shoulder at Jess, but the landgirl slept on, whether out of exhaustion or by some sea magic she did not know.

Lir moved one mighty arm, the one that held the conch, toward the land, and six of the mermen swam forward. Three of them, Dylan in the lead, hunched onto the beach. They moved awkwardly, pulling themselves along with their powerful arms. Melusina felt a fleeting shame for them, for on the land they had lost all of their grace.

Under Dylan's direction, the mermen bent low and put their hands under the dolphin, three mermen on each side. At a nod from the merrowman, they lifted the calf in their arms, cradled it. Melusina could see their muscles rippling with each movement. In the moonlight, the seawater dripping from their hair and rolling off their backs looked like the sweat of the landfolk.

Melusina felt herself strain with them and then could stay apart from them no longer. She ran up and cradled the dolphin's head in her hands and led them all back into the sea.

It was a slow pavane, a stately dance. Slower than it would have been, Melusina suddenly knew, with six strong landmen. With legs the seafolk could have walked the dolphin back to the sea.

But once the mermen had hunched and lurched

with the dolphin into the sea, no landman could have followed their liquid grace.

When they had launched the dolphin, Melusina stepped back to the shore. She stood and watched them. Lir called them to him with a wave of the conch. The men swam swiftly to his side. Dylan leaned over, placed his hand on Lir's, and whispered his words right into the king's hand.

Then they all stood on their tails so high, it seemed the moon was but a broken medallion on Lir's chest.

The old king nodded once at her, twice, then dove into the sea. The rest followed in a single movement. One minute they were there, ranged before her, an entire pod of merfolk; then they were gone.

Melusina moved backward, never taking her eyes off the place where the merfolk had disappeared. She felt a crystal tear start in her eye. She reached up and plucked it out, then hesitated a moment, turned and found the blanket where Jess still slept. She left the tear by Jess's cheek. Then she stood up and calmly walked back to the sea's edge.

She held her hands up over her head. "I am of the sea," she signed. "With legs or with tail, my blood is salt. Wait, my people. I am coming home."

And she dove, eel-slim, into a receding wave.

Sixteen

Jess had not slept easily. She was tired, but her conscience was still awake. So when the strange rustlings and gruntings of the mermen at work came to her as a slight vibration, she blinked her eyes awake. She was too tired to move, but her eyes watched it all as if it were a dream. She saw and felt everything that happened, but she understood only part of it.

She lay facing the sea and watched as Melusina stood before a host of shimmering people waiting far out on the waves. She watched as the six mermen hunched themselves along on their tails and picked the dolphin up from the beach. She watched as they brought him back to the sea, Melusina in the lead. And all the while, the seafolk stood, wavering on their tails under the summer moon. They waited and rocked with the sea's motion, the mermen with water-sleek muscles and the merwomen bare-breasted with strange flowers in their hair. And in the front, old and slim and tall, was a merman with a white beard, holding a conch shell.

As Jess watched, lying still as any sleeper, the

merfolk dived under and disappeared, and Melusina backed up to the blanket. That was when Jess closed her eyes. Because if Melusina had been punished before because of Jess's *seeing* her, Jess was certainly not going to let her know she had seen them *all* this time. So she closed her eyes. It was then she felt something plop gently by her cheek. She couldn't stand not knowing, and opened her eyes.

She was just in time to see Melusina walk to the water, raise her arms, and dive into a wave. But though she sat up and watched for a long time, Jess never saw her come up again.

"It was all a dream," Jess thought sleepily. She lay back down miserably on the blanket, and did not wake up again until dawn.

Dawn came, cold and silent. Jess awoke, shivered, sat up. Then she stood up, every muscle aching. She looked up the beach and then down.

There were tracks: Melusina's small feet and her own. There were some peculiar furrows alongside the spot where she remembered the dolphin lying. But there was no dolphin. There was no Melusina.

The tide was dead low.

She walked around for a few minutes, then came back to the sleeping bag and sat down slowly. She was still sitting there, surrounded by the detritus of the night, when the captain came home.

"So, she be gone," he said slowly. He seemed neither saddened nor surprised, just stepped out of his small boat and pulled it well up onto the beach.

Jess was appalled at his matter-of-fact tone. Then she tried to match it. "She's gone. Maybe drowned. Gone." Her voice was thick, but she managed to hold back her tears.

The old man sat down on the sleeping bag next to Jess. "Come now, gel," he said, trying to put his arm around her. "We didn't own her. Just borrowed her, like. You knew that all along. She came to teach us something, I expect. Them of the sea always has a lesson for us of the land. Here? What's this?" He reached his hand under his leg and held something up.

But Jess was paying no attention. "She didn't have to teach me anything. I didn't want to learn anything. I was happy enough before I met her. Nobody asked her to be my friend. I didn't want that. Because having a friend makes you . . . makes you. . . ." She couldn't find the word.

"Vulnerable?" The old man nodded his head. "A friend does that, gel. I knew that when I let you on me island." He patted her head awkwardly, as she turned over on her stomach and put her face in her hands, mumbling.

"What, gel? Speak up. My ears b'aint what they used to be. Used to be I could hear the wind."

She looked up at him, her eyes finally filling up with tears. "I saw her go. I saw them all."

"Did ye now," said the captain, but he listened carefully.

Jess sat up, her hands balled into fists. The old man took her fists, both of them, in one great cracked palm.

"And what did ye see, gel? Exactly now."

So Jess told him—about the dolphin and the touching and the Three Wisdoms and the merfolk all cast in silver moonlight, standing on their tails. And then she told him about Melusina turning back into one of them and diving into the sea.

"At least, I *think* I saw that," she finished lamely. "I'm not exactly sure if she got her tail back. And, of course, I might have dreamed it all. All of it. Even her. Even a friend."

The captain opened one of her fists and dropped something into it. "You didn't dream this," he said. "I found it there on the blanket. She left it for you, to show how much she cared, I be thinking. Friend to friend."

Jess looked and saw the crystal tear, gathering sunlight and showering her hand with rainbows. "You can have it, Captain. I don't want it. It will only remind me of . . . of everything that's gone."

"I'll keep it for a while then, gel. And with me own, the one she gave me, I'll make you a pair of rings, for those two funny ears of yours."

It was the only time the captain had ever directly referred to her deafness. Jess could feel the color rise in her cheeks. She couldn't think of a protest.

The old man went on as if he had not noticed her reaction. "For surely those two ears of yours be a help, a help to you the day we found the mermaid. Without 'em, how could you and she have talked? It be because of 'em ears, you talk with your hands. And without 'em ears, not you nor I could have helped that gel. Without 'em, how could you and she have been friends?"

Jess put her hands up to her ears and covered them. She had never thought of her ears as being a *help*. Only a burden. And certainly she had never thought they could get her a friend. With her hands over her ears, she heard a great roaring inside as if the sea were filling up her ears and inside her. She took her hands down and turned her face to the old man.

"Do it. Oh, Captain, do it. Make the earrings. And I'll wear them. I really will. I promise. I'll put my hair behind my ears and wear them. I'll show them to my mother and wear them. And Melusina will know. Somehow she *will* know."

"Yes, gel. And she'll get word to us, I expect. Though I be doubting we'll *see* her again."

Jess nodded solemnly. "We shouldn't *see* her again. It would be against the rules, the Three Wisdoms, really. And those Wisdoms, captain, why they'd work just as well here on land as down in the sea. Because they're true. Everyone should know them, not only where Melusina comes from. That much I know. And especially all the deaf kids. Because we are kind of like merfolk here on the land. Not really altogether fitting, speaking without tongues really. Knowing how much a touch means. And having that long patience."

Jess suddenly flung her arms out and gave the old man a rough hug. Then she jumped up and pulled him to his feet. Before he could ask what she wanted, she ran down to his boat and started unloading his supplies.

Far out in the cove, an old tortoise raised itself out of a wave. It lifted a flipper towards the shore. Jess saw it, recognized it, and held her hand up. She called out in her strange, thick, flat, unmusical voice. It floated over the water like a song. Her hand moved to mouth and head and then away. "Tell her we know. Tell her we knoooooooooow."

The turtle sank and did not come up again.

Jane Yolen is the author of many distinguished books, including *Greyling*, *The Emperor and the Kite*, and *The Girl Who Cried Flowers*, winner of the Golden Kite Award of the Society of Children's Book Writers, and a National Book Award finalist. She teaches creative writing, travels and lectures throughout the country, and lives on a farm in Massachusetts with her husband and children.

Laura Rader is a free-lance artist, illustrator, and toy designer. Born in Paterson, New Jersey, she studied at Pratt Institute of Art. Her work has appeared in magazines, but this is her first book. Mermaids and the sea were already haunting her consciousness and filling her sketchbooks, so it seemed almost a fulfillment of destiny when she was asked to illustrate *The Mermaid's Three Wisdoms*. Her drawings are done in a combination of pencil and ink. Ms. Rader now lives in Brooklyn.